Freedom School, Yes!

To the volunteers—A.L.

For Teyana—F.C.

Freedom School, Yes!

Amy Littlesugar
illustrated by Floyd Cooper

PHILOMEL BOOKS

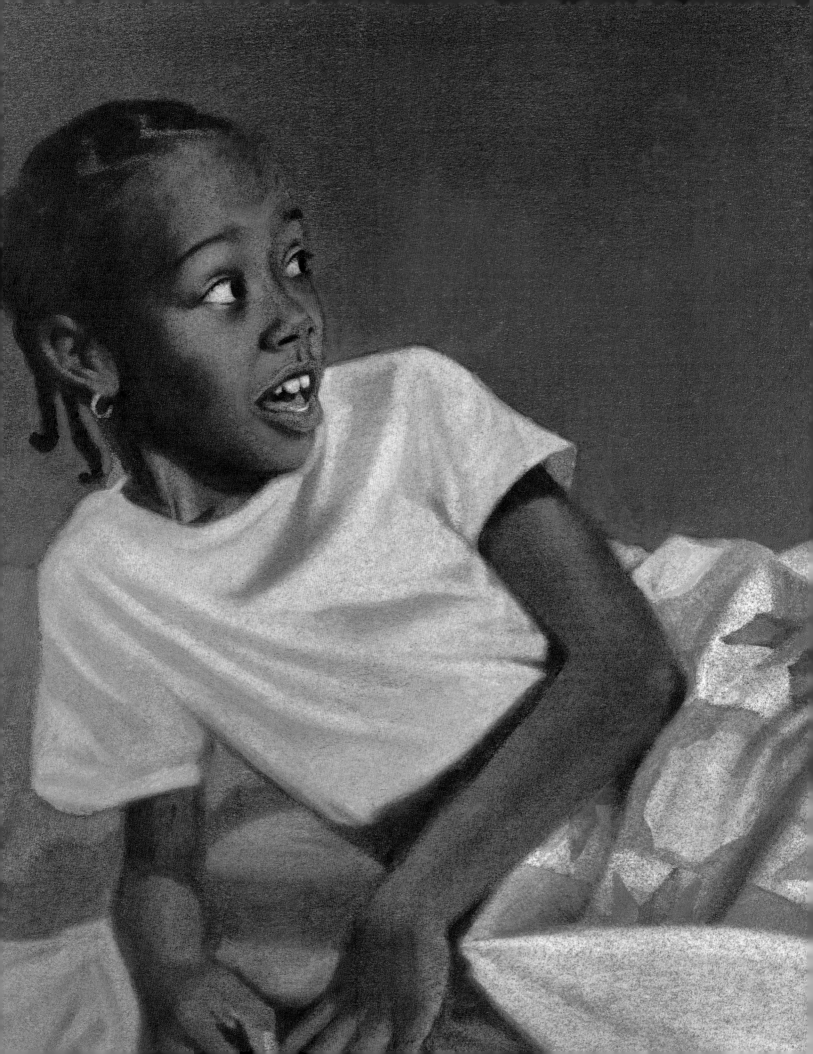

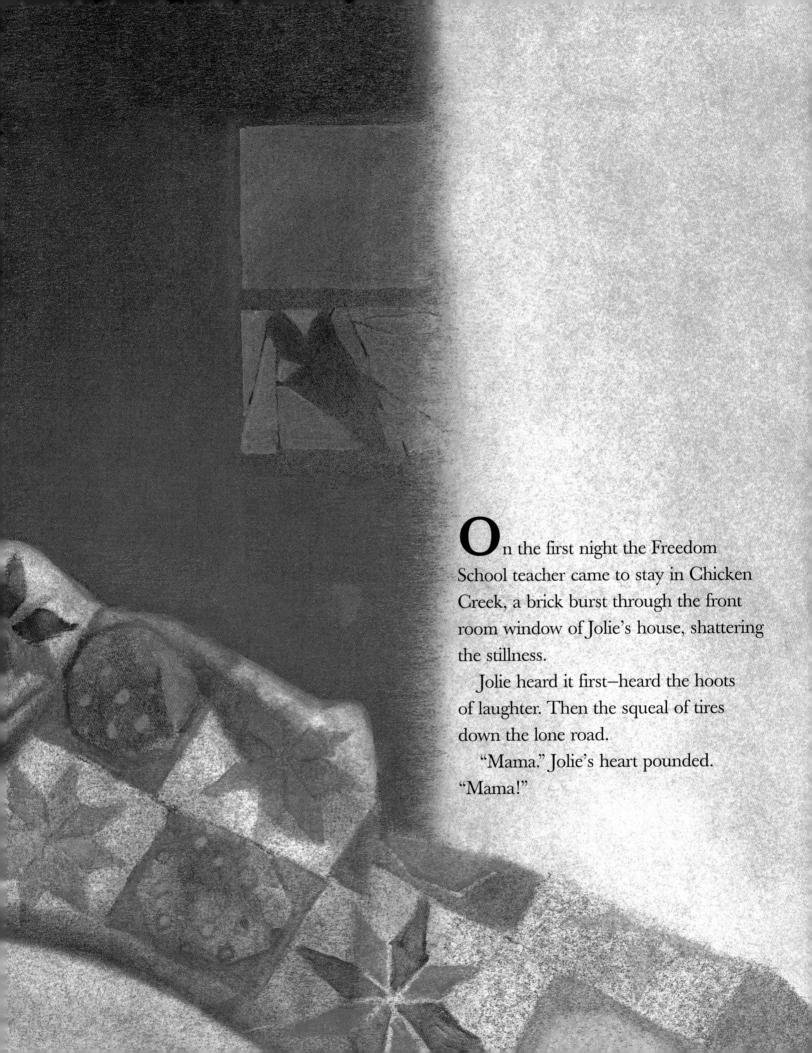

On the first night the Freedom School teacher came to stay in Chicken Creek, a brick burst through the front room window of Jolie's house, shattering the stillness.

Jolie heard it first—heard the hoots of laughter. Then the squeal of tires down the lone road.

"Mama." Jolie's heart pounded. "Mama!"

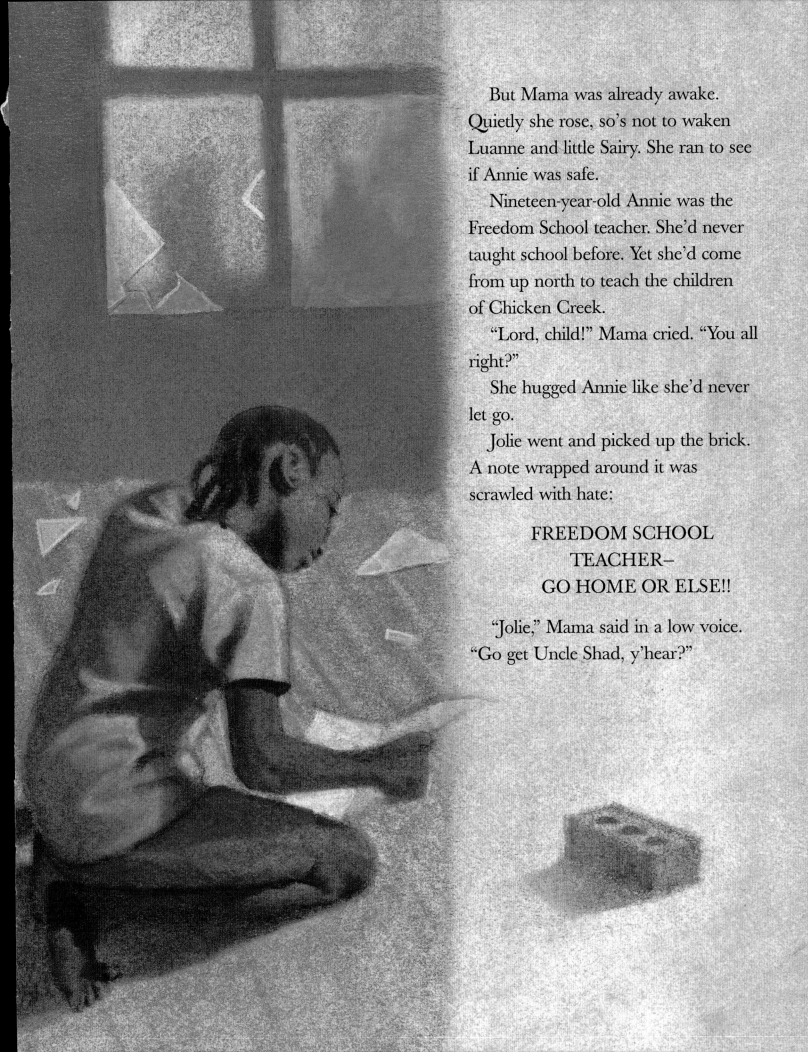

But Mama was already awake. Quietly she rose, so's not to waken Luanne and little Sairy. She ran to see if Annie was safe.

Nineteen-year-old Annie was the Freedom School teacher. She'd never taught school before. Yet she'd come from up north to teach the children of Chicken Creek.

"Lord, child!" Mama cried. "You all right?"

She hugged Annie like she'd never let go.

Jolie went and picked up the brick. A note wrapped around it was scrawled with hate:

**FREEDOM SCHOOL
TEACHER–
GO HOME OR ELSE!!**

"Jolie," Mama said in a low voice. "Go get Uncle Shad, y'hear?"

Jolie grabbed an old yellow bandanna, tied it round her head, and ran down the lone road. She heard the night wind in the cotton—Scratchety-scratch. Scratchety-scratch!

And she ran even faster.

Soon she came to the Mount Pleasant Church. Jolie remembered the Sunday Mama'd raised her hand, offering to let a Freedom School teacher come stay with them.

"Praise God!" Reverend Wilkins'd cried. And Jolie'd wanted to push Mama's hand right down. No one else'd raised theirs. No one. Just Mama.

By the time Jolie got to Uncle Shad's, tears were streaming down her face.

"Why, Sis!" Uncle Shad exclaimed
when he saw Jolie. "You okay? Your ma?
Luanne and Sairy?"

"Oh, Uncle Shad!" Jolie cried.
Then she told him all that'd
happened, and how she wished Annie'd
never come—nor Freedom School
neither.

Uncle Shad leaned both his hands
on his walking stick.

"Listen to me, Sis," he said quietly.
"This here Freedom School ain't gonna
be like no ordinary school. You gonna
learn 'bout people and places—'bout
who you are. Once you learn that, you
ain't gonna let bein' scared get in
your way."

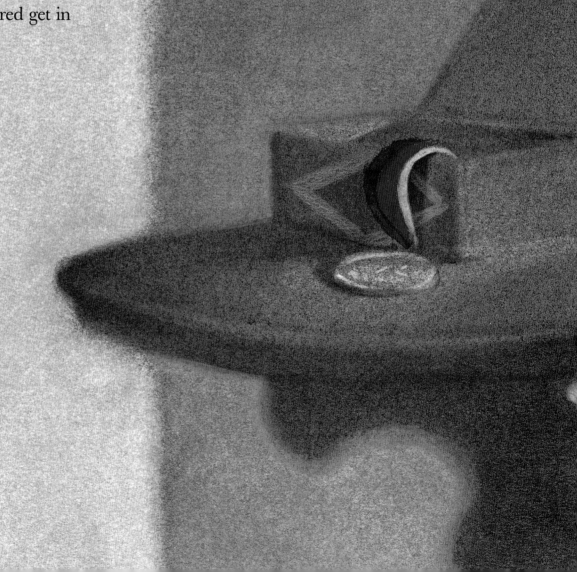

Next day was Sunday, and Annie was to meet the entire congregation at Mount Pleasant Church–where Freedom School would be.

"I hope you'll all send your children tomorrow," said Annie.

And some nodded shyly, pleased to know her. But others stayed away when she said, "Please just call me Annie."

Jolie knew they weren't used to calling a white woman by her first name. Annie ought to have known that!

That evening Mama washed and ironed school clothes, and everyone, even Annie, got a tub bath out back.

"Stop fidgetin'," Mama scolded as she braided Luanne's hair, then Sairy's, into a pinwheel of tiny braids.

When it was Annie's turn the girls oohed and ahhed. They'd never seen hair like that up close. So long and straight. Bright as a flame. Mama braided it up good and tight.

"There," she said. "Now it's Jolie's turn. Jolie!"

But Jolie wanted no part in it. She'd gone to sit on the old crate step, behind the orange trumpet vine. She looked up into a velvet sky, at the stars she loved. One day, Jolie imagined, she'd count them all.

She didn't need Freedom School for that.

Suddenly, though, a deep, bone-rattling sound crashed through Jolie's thoughts like thunder.

Mama and Annie were on the porch at once.

"Fire!" someone screamed. "The church is on fire!"

For hours the men and women of Chicken Creek, the young and the old, tried hard to save the burning church. But the hungry flames climbed higher and higher.

And by dawn it was hard to tell there'd ever been a church where the charred and smoking frame now stood.

Mama stood close to Annie and Jolie. Her voice sounded sad and empty.

"Guess there'll be no school tomorrow."

Then Reverend Wilkins did a surprising thing. Reaching his hands out to anyone who'd take them, he began to sing:

If I had a hammer,
I'd hammer in the morning.
I'd hammer in the evening—
all over this land!
I'd hammer out danger,
I'd hammer out a warning.
I'd hammer out love between
my brothers and my sisters,
all over this land!

And slowly, one by one, all those around Jolie joined in. Church or no church, even Jolie knew, there'd be Freedom School tomorrow.

It began under the shady branches of a hickory tree.

Now, not a lot of children came. Some were too scared. But enough for Annie to get to know—Roland Dodd, who was near fifteen, all the Christmas kids, and Althea and Essie, who were best friends. Jupiter Price was there, and he hated school.

Even Miss Rosetta came, and she was seventy. She brought a chair to set her old bones on and a coconut cake for Annie.

Then, on Tuesday, Reverend Wilkins brought good news. For one dollar—one dollar—a neighbor'd sold them a small piece of land. In no time they'd have a new church.

"And while we're at it," Reverend Wilkins said with a grin, "a brand-new Freedom School!"

All the next day axes and shovels flashed in the hot Chicken Creek sun. The temperature soared, but those who'd offered to build the church and school never stopped working.

Meanwhile, under that hickory tree with bees buzzing and birds chirping, Annie's class was learning so much, Miss Rosetta said it made her head spin—Jolie's too.

They learned about Jacob Lawrence, a black American artist whose paintings looked like stories. And Countee Cullen, a poet who wrote words like music.

What is Africa to me:
Copper sun or scarlet sea,
Jungle star and jungle track,
Strong bronzed me, or regal black...

Then Annie spoke of a free black man from long ago. "Benjamin Banneker was his name," she said. "He was a mathematician, a farmer, but more than anything else, he loved the stars."

And Jolie, twisting and twirling a blade of grass, listened and thought.

"Did he ever count all the stars?" she asked Annie that night. They sat on the front porch behind the orange trumpet vine.

"I don't know," Annie answered.

But Jolie felt sure Benjamin Banneker had.

By Saturday the church had a new
frame. And the school was almost done.
Soon it had a roof that reached to the
sky, sparkling new windows, and
a shiny door opened wide.

Before long it'd be ready for Annie's
class. But no chances were taken. Every
night someone took a turn guarding
the new buildings.

Annie'd wanted to, only Jolie
looked fearful.

"Are you afraid for me?"
Annie asked.

Jolie shook her head. But Annie
knew different. So she told Jolie
about a woman from slavery days
who'd risked her life helping
hundreds get free.

"Her name was Harriet Tubman,"
Annie said. "She was brave—
brave as a lion."

The days flew by. Jolie learned about people and places, just like Uncle Shad'd said. Once even the Mississippi Caravan of Music showed up. Jolie learned who Leadbelly was, and Big Bill Broonzy and "Ragtime" Texas.

"The blues is in each of you!" the guitar man sang.

Finally, the school was almost done. And on one of the last days of class under the hickory tree, Uncle Shad came.

"Pass this around for me, will you, Sis?" he asked Jolie. He handed her a fancy cigar box. It was Uncle Shad's silver medal! Carefully, Jolie showed it around. Even Jupiter Price craned his neck to see.

Uncle Shad told the class there'd been black heroes who'd fought for their country since America began. Men like Peter Salem and Crispus Attucks—"the first black men to die for independence."

Then Uncle Shad told how he'd been a soldier too, and wounded his leg saving a man's life. A white man's. Jolie sat very still, the medal warm in her hands. Uncle Shad went on. "Now I ain't even allowed to sit beside one at the lunch counter. Isn't that somethin'?"

He leaned both hands on his walking stick. "You all got to grow up and change that."

That night Annie took a turn guarding the school.

"I'll be fine." Annie smiled at Jolie, tweaking one braid. "Tell your mama I'll be back by supper."

But suppertime came and went, and twilight settled in.

"Where's Annie?" Mama worried.

"I'll find her, Mama," said Jolie.

"No, you won't, child," Mama warned.

Only Jolie didn't listen. When Mama's back was turned, she grabbed her old bandanna.

This time she wouldn't let being scared get in her way.

But shadows loomed ahead. Darkness came swirling in fast.

Jolie heard the night wind in the cotton. Scratchety-scratch. Scratchety-scratch! She almost turned back.

Then she heard something else. Something she'd heard before—hoots of laughter and the squeal of tires down the lone road out of Chicken Creek.

Jolie froze.

Annie! The school! Jolie began to run down the road faster than she ever thought she could.

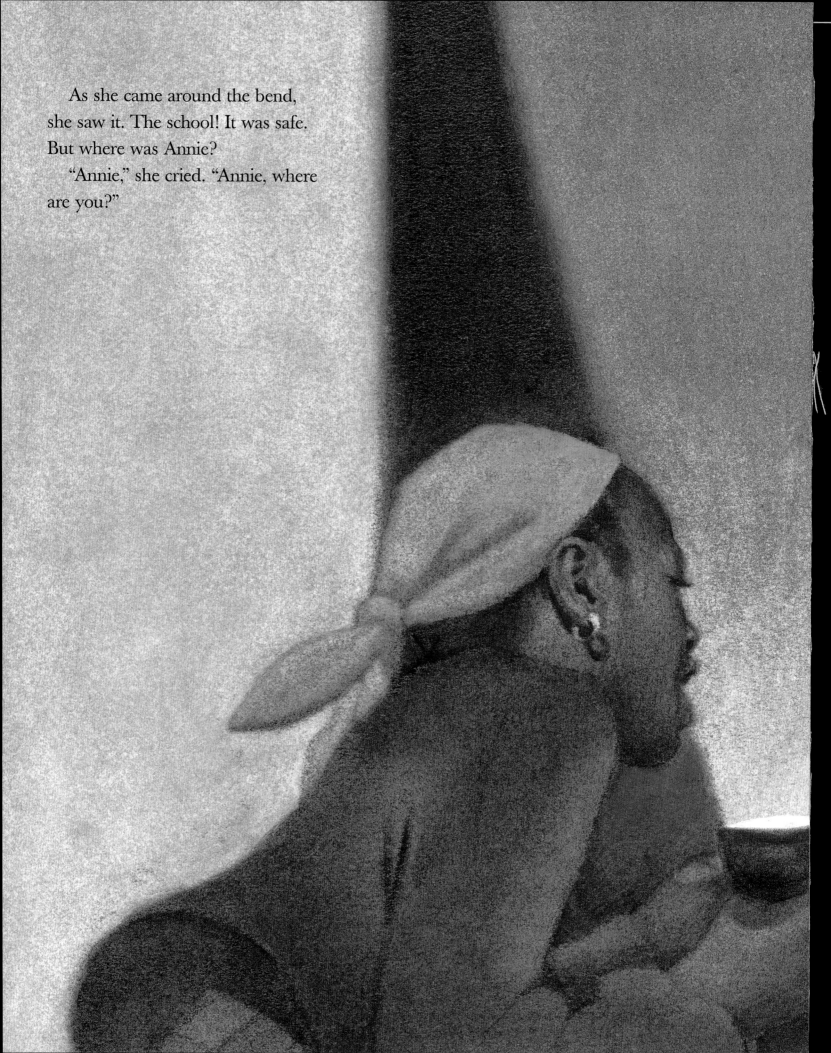

As she came around the bend,
she saw it. The school! It was safe.
But where was Annie?

"Annie," she cried. "Annie, where
are you?"

"I'm here, Jolie!" Annie's voice! "I thought I heard something—I was just checking the grounds."

Jolie tumbled into Annie's arms and could feel Annie's heart pounding. For the first time she realized how much the school—and Annie—meant to her.

"You were brave to come and find me, Jolie," Annie said. Then she smiled. "Brave as a lion."

Brave? Jolie wasn't sure, but she knew, standing there under the stars—Benjamin Banneker's stars—that when it came to school and learning, she was never going to let bein' scared get in her way again.

Author's Note

The 1964 Mississippi Summer Project involved more than 600 courageous young volunteers, black and white, who risked their lives to go south into the state of Mississippi, where the civil rights of black people had long been denied.

Some, such as Freedom School teacher Heather Booth, weren't more than eighteen years old. They, as well as the brave black families who took them into their homes that summer, faced incredible hostility and danger from local whites.

Yet the three Freedom School teachers I spoke with—Heather, Gren Whitman, and JoAnn Robinson—told me the risks were worth it. The volunteers taught thousands of black children and adults to read and write, and helped them register to vote for the first time. In the Freedom Schools, which mushroomed across Mississippi, black students at last learned about their own rich heritage.

I feel honored that Heather, Gren, and JoAnn allowed me to involve them in my story. I heard their voices with every word I wrote, and I'm glad for every child and adult who came to Freedom School that these courageous women were there during that special summer.

Bibliography

Adams, Russell L. *Great Negroes Past and Present*. Chicago: Afro-Am Publishing Corp., Inc., 1963.

Belfrage, Sally. *Freedom Summer*. New York: Viking, 1965.

Carawan, Guy, and Candie Carawan, eds. and comps. *Sing for Freedom: The Story of the Civil Rights Movement Through Its Songs*. Bethlehem, Pennsylvania: Sing Out Corp., 1960.

Charters, Samuel. *The Blues Makers*. New York: Da Capo Press, Inc., 1991.

Light, Ken. *Delta Time: Mississippi Photographs*. Washington, D.C.: Smithsonian Institution Press, 1995.

McAdam, Doug. *Freedom Summer*. New York: Oxford University Press, 1988.

Moody, Anne. *Coming of Age in Mississippi*. New York: Dial Press, 1968.

Seeger, Pete, and Bob Reiser. *Everybody Says Freedom*. New York: W. W. Norton & Company, 1989.

Sutherland, Elizabeth, ed. *Letters From Mississippi*. New York: McGraw Hill, 1965.

Welty, Eudora. *One Time, One Place: Mississippi in the Depression: A Snapshot Album*. Rev. ed. Jackson, Mississippi: University Press of Mississippi, 1996.

Conversations with the following Freedom School volunteers: Heather Tobis Booth, Grenville Whitman, JoAnn Robinson. And with Candie Carawan of the Highlander Research and Education Center in Mascot, Tennessee.

Thanks also to Doug McAdam, author of *Freedom Summer,* and Staughton Lynd, who was there!

PATRICIA LEE GAUCH, EDITOR

Philomel Books, a division of Penguin Putnam Books for Young Readers, 345 Hudson Street, New York, NY, 10014.
Philomel Books, Reg. U.S. Pat. & Tm. Off. Published simultaneously in Canada. Manufactured in China by South China Printing Co. (1988) Ltd. Book design by Sharon Murray Jacobs. The text is set in 14-point Baskerville Book.
Library of Congress Cataloging-in-Publication Data Littlesugar, Amy. Freedom school, yes! / Amy Littlesugar, Floyd Cooper. p. cm. Summary: When their house is attacked because her mother volunteered to take in the young white woman who has come to teach black children at the Freedom School, Jolie is afraid, but she overcomes her fear after learning the value of education. 1. Mississippi Freedom Schools–Juvenile fiction. [1. Mississippi Freedom Schools–Fiction. 2. Afro-Americans–Fiction. 3. Mississippi–Race relations–Fiction. 4. Schools–Fiction.] I. Cooper, Floyd. II. Title. PZ7.L7362 Fr 2000 [E]–dc21 99-049706 ISBN 0-399-23006-8
10 9 8 7 6 5 4